Frank E. Bliss, Press De Vinne

An Antidote Against Melancholy

Compounded of Choice Poems, Jovial Songs, Merry Ballads, and...

Frank E. Bliss, Press De Vinne

An Antidote Against Melancholy
Compounded of Choice Poems, Jovial Songs, Merry Ballads, and...

ISBN/EAN: 9783744764544

Printed in Europe, USA, Canada, Australia, Japan

Cover: Foto ©Andreas Hilbeck / pixelio.de

More available books at **www.hansebooks.com**

An Antidote

against

MELANCHOLY

Compounded of *Choice Poems, Jovial Songs,*
Merry Ballads, and *Witty Parodies.*
Moſt pleasant and diverting to read.

AT NEW-YORK.

Printed by T. L. D. V. *for* PRATT MANUFACT-
URING COMPANY, *and are to be had at their*
shop in Broadway, No. 46, near Bowling Green.

CHRISTMAS, MDCCCLXXXIV.

To the
READER.

COURTEOUS READER:

THY grateful reception of our former collection hath induced us to a second essay of the same nature; and, as we are confident it will be found in no wise inferiour to the former in worth, so we assure ourselves it shall at least equal it in its fortunate acceptation. It being our design rather to make such a collection as shall please all Complexions, Ages, and Constitutions of either Sexes, than to gratify our vanity by a display of learning, there will be found here poems of all kinds, pastoral, lyric, convivial, grave, and gay, but none to offend any. To gather these poems, for many of which we have gone to the original sources, has been a long undertaking; but if only this little book, which we now present to thee, shall make good its claim to being An Antidote Against Melancholy, though to but one of its readers, we shall feel that our labour has been sufficiently rewarded. We have of purpose kept the number of these, our selections, within small compass, preferring to serve up these delicates by frugal messes, as aiming at thy satisfaction, not satiety. But our design being more upon thy judgment than thy patience, more to delight thee than to detain thee by a tedious (and we fear seldom-read) epistle, we will draw the curtain that shuts from thy view what we have prepared; first, however, acknowledging our obligation to HENRY HOLT & CO., CHARLES SCRIBNER'S SONS, and WHITE, STOKES & ALLEN for courtesies extended during the compilation of this work. Finally, there remains but the pleasant duty of returning grateful thanks for thy patronage in the past, and of wishing thee a Merrie Christmas.

Thy much obliged, and

Most obedient servants,

The Publishers.

Cast care away, let sorrow cease,
A fig for melancholy!
Let 's laugh and sing, or, if you please,
We 'll frolic with sweet Dolly.
Old English Song.

CORIDON'S SONG.

THOMAS LODGE,
1557?–1625?

From " Rosalynde : Euphues Golden Legacie, by T. L. Gent. London, 1592." It was this Pastoral Romance that afforded Shakspere the hints for his exquisite Comedy of "As You Like It."

A BLITHE and bonny country-lass,
　　Heigh ho, bonny lass ;
Sate sighing on the tender grass,
　　And weeping said : Will none come woo me ?
A smicker boy, a lither swain,
　　Heigh ho, a smicker swain ;
That in his love was wanton fain,
　　With smiling looks straight came unto her.

When as the wanton wench espied,
　　Heigh ho, when she espied
The means to make herself a bride,
　　She simpered smooth like bonny-bell.
The swain that saw her squint-eyed kind,
　　Heigh ho, squint-eyed kind ;
His arms about her body twined,
　　And said : Fair lass, how fare ye, well ?

The country kit said: Well, forsooth,
 Heigh ho, well, forsooth;
But that I have a longing tooth,
 A longing tooth that makes me cry;
Alas (said he), what gars thy grief?
 Heigh ho, what gars thy grief?
A wound (quoth she) without relief,
 I fear a maid that I shall die.

If that be all, the Shepherd said,
 Heigh ho, the Shepherd said;
I 'll make thee wive it, gentle maid,
 And so recure thy maladie:
Hereon they kiss'd with many an oath,
 Heigh ho, many an oath;
And 'fore god Pan did plight their troth,
 So to the church apace they hie.

And God send every pretty peate,
 Heigh ho, the pretty peate,
That fears to die of this conceit,
 So kind a friend to help at last:
Then maids shall never long again,
 Heigh ho, to long again;
When they find ease for such a pain,
 Thus my roundelay is past.

THE SHEPHERD'S DAFFODIL.

MICHAEL DRAYTON,
1563–1631.

The following stanzas, by Michael Drayton, are found in one of his Pastorals, bearing the whimsical title of "Idea. The Shepheard's Garland, fashioned in nine Eclogs. Rowland's Sacrifice to the Nine Muses," 1593. This song occurs in the Ninth Eclogue.

BATTE.— GORBO as thou cam'st this way
　　By yonder little hill,
Or as thou through the fields did'st stray,
　　Saw'st thou my *Daffodil?*

She 's in a frock of *Lincoln* green,
　　Which colour likes her sight,
And never hath her beauty seen
　　But through a veil of white.

Than roses richer to behold
　　That trim up lovers' bowers,
The pansy and the marigold,
　　Though Phœbus' paramours.

GORBO.—Thou well describ'st the Daffodil;
　　It is not full an hour
Since by the spring near yonder hill
　　I saw that lovely flower.

BATTE.—Yet my fair flower thou did'st not meet
  Nor news of her did'st bring,
  And yet my *Daffodil* 's more sweet
  Than that by yonder spring.

GORBO.—I saw a shepherd that does keep
  In yonder field of lilies,
  Was making (as he fed his sheep)
  A wreath of daffodillies.

BATTE.—Yet, *Gorbo*, thou delud'st me still;
  My flower thou did'st not see,
  For, know, my pretty *Daffodil*
  Is worn of none but me.

To show itself but near her feet
  No lily is so bold,
  Except to shade her from the heat
  Or keep her from the cold.

GORBO.—Through yonder vale as I did pass,
  Descending from the hill,
  I met a smirking bonny lass;
  They call her *Daffodil.*

Whose presence as along she went
  The pretty flowers did greet,
  As though their heads they downward bent
  With homage to her feet.

And all the shepherds that were nigh,
From top of every hill
Unto the valleys loud did cry
"There goes sweet *Daffodil*."

BATTE.—Aye, gentle shepherd, now with joy
Thou all my flocks dost fill;
That 's she alone, kind shepherd's boy;
Let us to *Daffodil*.

LULLABY SONG.

UNCERTAIN.

From " The Pleasant Comodie of Patient Gris-sill." 1603. By Thomas Dekker, Henry Chettle, and William Haughton.

GOLDEN slumbers kiss your eyes,
   Smiles awake you when you rise;
Sleep, pretty wantons, do not cry,
   And I will sing a lullaby.

Care is heavy, therefore sleep you,
   You are care, and care must keep you;
Sleep, pretty wantons, do not cry,
   And I will sing a lullaby,
      Rock them, rock them, lullaby.

A DITTY.

SIR PHILIP SIDNEY,
1554–1586.

Quoted by George Puttenham in his "Arte of English Poesy, 1589," as an instance of "Epimone, or the Love Burden." In the "Arcadia, 1598," however, these lines appear as a sonnet by the omission of the refrain as here, and the addition of six lines; the final one being the refrain.

M Y true love hath my heart, and I have his,
By just exchange one to the other given:
I hold his dear, and mine he cannot miss,
There never was a better bargain driven:
My true love hath my heart, and I have his.

His heart in me keeps him and me in one,
My heart in him his thoughts and senses guides:
He loves my heart, for once it was his own,
I cherish his because in me it abides:
My true love hath my heart, and I have his.

DRINKING SONG.

JOHN STILL?
1543-1607.

This excellent old Drinking Song, which Warton terms " the first chanson à boire of any merit in our language," is from " A ryght pithy, pleasaunt, and merie Comedie: Intytuled Gammer Gurton's Nedle." London, 1575.

I CANNOT eat but little meat,
　　My stomach is not good;
But sure, I think that I can drink
　　With him that wears a hood.
Tho' I go bare, take ye no care,
　　I am nothing a cold,
I stuff my skin so full within
　　Of jolly good ale and· old.

　　Back and side go bare, go bare,
　　　Both foot and hand go cold;
　　But, belly, God send thee good ale enough,
　　　Whether it be new or old.

I love no roast but a nut-brown toast,
　　And a crab[1] laid in the fire;
A little bread shall do me stead,
　　Much bread I not desire.

---

[1] Crab-apple.

No frost, nor snow, nor wind, I trow,
  Can hurt me if I wold,[1]
I am so wrapt, and throwly[2] lapt
  Of jolly good ale and old.
    Back and side go bare, etc.

And Tib, my wife, that as her life
  Loveth well good ale to seek,
Full oft drinks she, till ye may see
  The tears run down her cheek :
Then doth she troul to me the bowl,
  Even as a maltworm should,
And saith, "Sweetheart, I took my part
  Of this jolly good ale and old."
    Back and side go bare, etc.

Now let them drink till they nod and wink,
  Even as good fellows should do ;
They shall not miss to have the bliss
  Good ale doth bring men to ;
And all poor souls that have scoured bowls,
  Or have them lustily troul'd,
God save the lives of them and their wives,
  Whether they be young or old.
    Back and side go bare, etc.

---

[1] Willed.   [2] Thoroughly.

DEATH'S FINAL CONQUEST.

JAMES SHIRLEY,
1596-1666.

*These fine moral stanzas were originally in-
tended for a solemn funeral song in " The
Contention of Ajax and Ulysses."   1659.   It
is said to have been a favorite song with King
Charles II.*

THE glories of our birth and state
   Are shadows, not substantial things;
There is no armour against fate;
   Death lays his icy hands on kings:
     Sceptre and crown
     Must tumble down,
And in the dust be equal made
With the poor crooked scythe and spade.

Some men with swords may reap the field,
   And plant fresh laurels where they kill:
But their strong nerves at last must yield,
   They tame but one another still.
     Early or late,
     They stoop to fate,
And must give up their murm'ring breath
When the pale captive creeps to death.

The laurel withers on your brow,
  Then boast no more your mighty deeds,
Upon Death's purple altar now
  See where the victor victim bleeds;
      All heads must come
      To the cold tomb:
Only the actions of the just
Smell sweet, and blossom in the dust.

A GENTLEMAN OF THE OLD SCHOOL.

AUSTIN DOBSON,
Born 1840.

From " Old-World Idylls, 1883."   Mr. Dobson belongs to that recent class of English poets who have reproduced the old French forms of verse in the rondeau, virelai, villanelle, ballade, etc.

HE lived in that past Georgian day,
   When men were less inclined to say
That "Time is Gold," and overlay
      With toil their pleasure;
He held some land, and dwelt thereon,—
Where, I forget,—the house is gone;
His Christian name, I think, was John,—
      His surname, Leisure.

Reynolds has painted him,— a face
Filled with a fine, old-fashioned grace,
Fresh-coloured, frank, with ne'er a trace
      Of trouble shaded;
The eyes are blue, the hair is drest
In plainest way,— one hand is prest
Deep in a flapped canary vest,
      With buds brocaded.

He wears a brown old Brunswick coat,
With silver buttons,— round his throat,
A soft cravat; — in all you note
        An elder fashion.
A strangeness, which, to us who shine
In shapely hats,— whose coats combine
All harmonies of hue and line,
        Inspires compassion.

He lived so long ago, you see!
Men were untravelled then, but we,
Like Ariel, post o'er land and sea
        With careless parting;
He found it quite enough for him
To smoke his pipe in "garden trim,"
And watch, about the fish-tank's brim,
        The swallows darting.

He liked the well-wheel's creaking tongue,—
He liked the thrush that stopped and sung,—
He liked the drone of flies among
        His netted peaches.
He liked to watch the sunlight fall
Athwart his ivied orchard wall;
Or pause to catch the cuckoo's call
        Beyond the beeches.

His were the times of Paint and Patch,
And yet no Ranelagh could match
The sober doves that round his thatch
        Spread tails and sidled;

He liked their ruffling, puffed content,—
For him their drowsy wheelings meant
More than a Mall of Beaux that bent
        Or Belles that bridled.

Not that, in truth, when life began
He shunned the flutter of the fan ;
He, too, had maybe "pinked his man"
        In Beauty's quarrel;
But now his "fervent youth" had flown
Where lost things go ; and he was grown
As staid and slow-paced as his own
        Old hunter, Sorrel.

Yet still he loved the chase, and held
That no composer's score excelled
The merry horn, when Sweetlip swelled
        Its jovial riot;
But most his measured words of praise
Caressed the angler's easy ways,—
His idly meditative days,—
        His rustic diet.

Not that his "meditating" rose
Beyond a sunny summer doze;
He never troubled his repose
        With fruitless prying;
But held, as law for high and low,
What God withholds no man can know,
And smiled away inquiry so,
        Without replying.

We read — alas, how much we read! —
The jumbled strifes of creed and creed
With endless controversies feed
       Our groaning tables;
His books — and they sufficed him — were
Cotton's " Montaigne," " The Grave " of Blair,
A " Walton "— much the worse for wear,
       And "Æsop's Fables."

One more,— " The Bible." Not that he
Had searched its page as deep as we ;
No sophistries could make him see
       Its slender credit ;
It may be that he could not count
The sires and sons to Jesse's fount,—
He liked the " Sermon on the Mount,"—
       And more, he read it.

Once he had loved, but failed to wed,
A red-cheeked lass, who long was dead ;
His ways were far too slow, he said,
       To quite forget her;
And still, when time had turned him gray
The earliest hawthorn buds in May
Would find his lingering feet astray,
       Where first he met her.

"*In Cœlo Quies*" heads the stone
On Leisure's grave,—now little known,
A tangle of wild-rose has grown
       So thick across it ;

The " Benefactions " still declare
He left the clerk an elbow-chair,
And "Twelve Pence Yearly to Prepare
          A Christmas Posset."

Lie softly, Leisure!   Doubtless you,
With too serene a conscience drew
Your easy breath, and slumbered through
          The gravest issue;
But we, to whom our age allows
Scarce space to wipe our weary brows,
Look down upon your narrow house,
          Old friend, and miss you!

"FAIR AMORET IS GONE ASTRAY."

WILLIAM CONGREVE,
1670–1729.

FAIR Amoret is gone astray,
    Pursue, and seek her, every lover;
I 'll tell the signs by which you may
    The wandering shepherdess discover.

Coquet and coy at once her air,
    Both studied, tho' both seem neglected;
Careless she is, with artful care,
    Affecting to seem unaffected.

With skill her eyes dart every glance,
    Yet change so soon you 'd ne'er suspect them;
For she 'd persuade they wound by chance,
    Though certain aim and art direct them.

She likes herself, yet others hates
    For that which in herself she prizes;
And, while she laughs at them, forgets
    She is the thing that she despises.

ON WOMEN.

Unknown.

*From " Wit's Recreations, Augmented with
ingenious conceites for the Wittie, and Merrie
medecines for the Melancholie. 1640."*

WOMEN are books, and men the readers be,
In whom oft times they great Errata see;
Here sometimes we a blot, there we espy
A leaf misplac'd, at least a line awry;
If they are books, I wish that my wife were
An almanack, to change her every year.

SONG.

SIR CHARLES SEDLEY,
1639–1701.

Macaulay speaks of Sir Charles Sedley as " one of the most brilliant and profligate wits of the Restoration." He was the author of three plays, " The Mulberry Garden," 1668; "Antony and Cleopatra," 1677; and "Bellamira," 1687.

PHYLLIS, men say that all my vows
    Are to thy fortune paid ;
Alas, my heart he little knows
. Who thinks my love a trade.

Were I of all these woods the lord,
    One berry from thy hand
More real pleasure would afford
    Than all my large command.

THE COUNTRY LASS.

MARTIN PARKER.

It would be difficult to name many ballads which have had a larger share of popularity than "The Country Lass." It was first printed for the Assigns of Thomas Symcocke, about 1620; and was the composition of Martin Parker, a popular writer of ballads of that time.

To a daintie new note, which if you can hit,
There's another tune will as well fit.
That's the mother beguiles the daughter.

ALTHOUGH I am a country lass,
   A lofty mind I bear—a,
I think myself as good as those
   That gay apparel wear—a,
My coat is made of homely gray,
   Yet is my skin as soft — a,
As those that with the chiefest wines
   Do bathe their bodies oft — a.
   Down, down, derry, derry down,
     Heigh down, a down, a down a,
   A derry, derry, derry, derry, down,
     Heigh down, a down, a derry.

What, though I keep my father's sheep ?
  A thing that must be done — a,
A garland of the fairest flowers
  Shall shroud me from the sun — a,
And when I see them feeding be,
  Where grass and flowers spring — a,
Close by a crystal fountain side,
  I sit me down, and sing — a.
    Down, down, derry, derry down, etc.

Dame Nature crowns us with delight,
  Surpassing court or city,
We pleasures take from morn to night,
  In sports and pastimes pretty :
Your city dames in coaches ride
  Abroad for recreation,
We country lasses hate their pride,
  And keep the country fashion.
    Down, down, derry, derry down, etc.

Your city wives lead wanton lives,
  And if they come i' th' country,
They are so proud, that each one strives
  For to outbrave our gentry.
We country lasses homely be ;
  For seat nor wall we strive not ;
We are content with our degree ;
  Our debtors we deprive not.
    Down, down, derry, derry down, etc.

I care not for a fan or mask,
  When Titan's heat reflecteth,
A homely hat is all I ask,
  Which well my face protecteth ;

Yet am I in my country guise,
  Esteemèd lass as pretty,
As those that every day devise
  New shapes in court and city.
    Down, down, derry, derry down, etc.

In every season of the year
  I undergo my labour,—
No shower, nor wind, at all I fear,
  My limbs I do not favour;
If summer's heat my beauty stain,
  It makes me ne'er the sicker,
Sith I can wash it off again
  With a cup of Christmas liquor.
    Down, down, derry, derry down, etc.

SECOND PART.

At Christmas time, in mirth and glee,
  I dance with young men neatly,
And who i' th' city like to me,
  Shall pleasure taste completely?
No sport, but pride and luxury
  I' th' city can be found then,
But bounteous hospitality
  I' th' country doth abound then.
    Down, down, derry, derry down, etc.

I' th' Spring my labour yields delight
  To walk i' th' merry morning,
When Flora is (to please my sight)
  The ground with flowers adorning;

With merry lads to make the hay
    I go, and do not grumble,
My work doth seem to be but play,
    When with young men I tumble.
        Down, down, derry, derry down, etc.

The lark and thrush from briar to bush
    Do leap, and skip and sing — a,
And all is then to welcome in
    The long and look'd for Spring — a;
We fear not Cupid's arrows keen,
    Dame Venus we defy — a,
Diana is our honour'd queen,
    And her we magnify — a.
        Down, down, derry, derry down, etc.

That which your city damsels scorn,
    We hold our chiefest jewel,
Without, to work at hay and corn,
    Within, to bake and brew well;
To keep the dairy decently,
    And all things clean and neatly,
Your city minions do defy,—
    Their scorn we weigh not greatly.
        Down, down, derry, derry down, etc.

When we together a milking go
    With pails upon our heads — a,
And walking over woods and fields,
    Where grass and flowers spread — a,

3

In honest pleasure we delight,
  Which makes our labour sweet — a,
And mirth exceeds on every side
  When lads and lassies meet — a.
    Down, down, derry, derry down, etc.

Then do not scorn a country lass,
  Though she be plain and meanly,
Who takes a country wench to wife
  (That goeth neat and cleanly)
Is better sped, than if he wed
  A fine one from the city;
For there they are so nicely bred,
  They must not work for pity.
    Down, down, derry, derry down, etc.

I speak not this to that intent
  (As some may well conjecture),
As though to wooing I were bent,—
  No, I ne'er learn'd Love's lecture;
But what I sing is in defence
  Of all plain country lasses,
Whose modest, honest innocence
  All city girls surpasses.
    Down, down, derry, derry down,
      Heigh down, a down, a down a,
    A derry, derry, derry, derry down,
      Heigh down, a down, a derry.

WINIFREDA.

UNKNOWN.

" This beautiful address to conjugal love," says Bishop Percy, " a subject too much neglected by the libertine Muses, was, I believe, first printed in a volume of ' Miscellaneous Poems, by Several hands, published by D. Lewis, 1726, 8vo '." The authorship is unknown, though it has been ascribed, probably erroneously, to Gilbert Cooper.

A WAY; let nought to love displeasing,
　My Winifreda, move your care;
Let nought delay the heavenly blessing,
　Nor squeamish pride, nor gloomy fear.

What though no grants of royal donors
　With pompous titles grace our blood;
We'll shine in more substantial honors,
　And to be noble we'll be good.　·

Our name, while virtue thus we tender,
　Will sweetly sound where e'er 't is spoke;
And all the great ones they shall wonder
　How they respect such little folk.

What though from fortune's lavish bounty
　No mighty treasures we possess;
We'll find within our pittance plenty,
　And be content without excess.

Still shall each returning season
   Sufficient for our wishes give;
For we will live a life of reason,
   And that 's the only life to live.

Through youth and age in love excelling,
   We 'll hand in hand together tread;
Sweet-smiling peace shall crown our dwelling,
   And babes, sweet-smiling babes, our bed.

How should I love the pretty creatures,
   While round my knees they fondly clung;
To see them look their mother's features,
   To hear them lisp their mother's tongue.

And when with envy time transported,
   Shall think to rob us of our joys,
You 'll in your girls again be courted,
   And I 'll go wooing in my boys.

THE VICAR OF BRAY.

UNKNOWN.

Nichols, in his Select Poems, says that the Song of the Vicar of Bray " was written by a soldier in Colonel Fuller's troop of Dragoons, in the reign of George I."

IN good King Charles's golden days,
  When loyalty no harm meant,
A zealous high-church-man I was,
  And so I got preferment.
To teach my flock I never miss'd,
  Kings are by God appointed;
And damn'd are those that do resist,
  Or touch the Lord's Anointed.
    And this is law, I will maintain,
      Until my dying day, sir,
    That whatsoever king shall reign,
    I'll be the Vicar of Bray, sir.

When Royal James obtain'd the crown,
  And popery came in fashion,
The penal laws I hooted down,
  And read the Declaration:

The Church of Rome I found would fit
  Full well my constitution;
And had become a Jesuit,
  But for the Revolution.
    And this is law, etc.

When William was our King declar'd,
  To ease the nation's grievance,
With this new wind about I steer'd
  And swore to him allegiance:
Old principles I did revoke,
  Set conscience at a distance;
Passive obedience was a joke,
  A jest was non-resistance.
    And this is law, etc.

When gracious Anne became our queen,
  The Church of England's glory,
Another face of things was seen,
  And I became a tory!
Occasional conformists base,
  I damn'd their moderation;
And thought the church in danger was,
  By such prevarication.
    And this is law, etc.

When George in pudding-time came o'er,
  And moderate men looked big, sir,
I turn'd a cat-in-pan once more,
  And so became a whig, sir,

And thus preferment I procur'd
  From our new faiths-defender;
And almost ev'ry day abjur'd
  The Pope and the Pretender.
    And this is law, etc.

Th' illustrious house of Hanover,
  And Protestant succession;
To these I do allegiance swear—
  While they can keep possession:
For in my faith and loyalty,
  I never more will faulter,
And George my lawful king shall be —
  Until the times do alter.
    And this is law, I will maintain,
      Until my dying day, sir,
    That whatsoever king shall reign,
      I'll be the Vicar of Bray, sir.

MY GRANDMOTHER.

(SUGGESTED BY A PICTURE BY MR. ROMNEY.)

FREDERICK LOCKER,
Born 1821.

From " London Lyrics. 1862." Mr. Locker is one of the most delightful of the English writers of "vers de societé," and his poems may be read with pleasure, for his gayety is always sweet and genial.

T HIS relative of mine
    Was she seventy and nine
      When she died?
By the canvas may be seen
How she looked at seventeen,—
      As a bride.

Beneath a summer tree
As she sits, her reverie
      Has a charm;
Her ringlets are in taste,—
What an arm! and what a waist
      For an arm!

In bridal coronet,
Lace, ribbons, and *coquette*
      Falbala;
Were Romney's limning true,
What a lucky dog were you,
      Grandpapa!

Her lips are sweet as love,—
They are parting! Do they move?
        Are they dumb?—
Her eyes are blue, and beam
Beseechingly, and seem
        To say, " Come."

What funny fancy slips
From atween these cherry lips?
        Whisper me,
Sweet deity, in paint,
What canon says I may n't
        Marry thee?

That good-for-nothing Time
Has a confidence sublime!
        When I first
Saw this lady, in my youth,
Her winters had, forsooth,
        Done their worst.

Her locks (as white as snow)
Once shamed the swarthy crow.
        By-and-by,
That fowl's avenging sprite
Set his cloven foot for spite
        In her eye.

Her rounded form was lean,
And her silk was bombazine :—
        Well I wot,
With her needles would she sit,
And for hours would she knit,—
        Would she not?

Ah, perishable clay !
Her charms had dropt away
    One by one.
But if she heaved a sigh
With a burthen, it was "Thy
    Will be done."

In travail, as in tears,
With the fardel of her years
    Overprest,—
In mercy was she borne
Where the weary ones and worn
    Are at rest.

I 'm fain to meet you there,—
If as witching as you were,
    Grandmamma !
This nether world agrees
That the better it must please
    Grandpapa.

O NANCY WILT THOU GO WITH ME?

THOMAS PERCY,
1728–1811.

The following very lovely song is the composition of Bishop Percy, the well-known editor of the Reliques of Ancient English Poetry. Burns, writing of this song, remarks, It is "perhaps the most beautiful ballad in the English language."

O NANCY, wilt thou go with me,
　　Nor sigh to leave the flaunting town?
Can silent glens have charms for thee,
　　The lowly cot and russet gown?
No longer drest in silken sheen,
　　No longer deck'd with jewels rare,
Say, canst thou quit each courtly scene,
　　Where thou wert fairest of the fair?

O Nancy! when thou 'rt far away,
　　Wilt thou not cast a wish behind?
Say, canst thou face the parching ray,
　　Nor shrink before the wintry wind?
O, can that soft and gentle mien
　　Extremes of hardships learn to bear,
Nor sad regret each courtly scene,
　　Where thou wert fairest of the fair?

O Nancy, canst thou love so true,
  Through perils keen with me to go,
Or when thy swain mishap shall rue,
  To share with him the pang of woe?
Say, should disease or pain befall,
  Wilt thou assume the nurse's care
Nor wistful those gay scenes recall,
  Where thou wert fairest of the fair?

And when at last thy love shall die,
  Wilt thou receive his parting breath?
Wilt thou repress each struggling sigh,
  And cheer with smiles the bed of death?
And wilt thou o'er his breathless clay
  Strew flowers, and drop the tender tear,
Nor then regret those scenes so gay
  Where thou wert fairest of the fair?

A PARODY.

REV. R. H. BARHAM,
1788–1845.

*The Rev. Charles Wolfe's immortal Ode, "The
Burial of Sir John Moore," was first published anonymously in "Currick's Morning
Post" (Ireland), in 1815; and though it at
once became widely popular, its authorship
long remained the subject of controversy.
Among the numerous claimants to the authorship was a certain soi-disant "Doctor,"
a veterinary surgeon of the name of Marshall; and it was to expose and ridicule his
pretensions that the following excellent parody
was written by the Rev. R. H. Barham.
"Doctor" Marshall was more remarkable
for convivial than literary tastes.*

NOT a *sou* had he got, not a guinea or note,
    And he looked confoundedly flurried,
As he bolted away without paying his shot,
    And the landlady after him hurried.

We saw him again at dead of night,
    When home from the club returning,
We "twigg'd" the Doctor beneath the light
    Of the gas-lamp brilliantly burning.

All bare, and exposed to the midnight dews,
    Reclined in the gutter we found him,
And he look'd like a gentleman taking a snooze,
    With his *Marshall* cloak around him.

"The Doctor 's as drunk as the d——," we said,
  And we managed a shutter to borrow;
We raised him, and sigh'd at the thought that his head
  Would consumedly ache on the morrow.

We bore him home, and we put him to bed,
  And we told his wife and his daughter
To give him, next morning, a couple of red
  Herrings, with soda water.

Loudly they talk'd of his money that 's gone,
  And his lady began to upbraid him;
But little he reck'd, so they let him snore on
  'Neath the counterpane just as we laid him.

We tuck'd him in, and had hardly done,
  When, beneath the window calling,
We heard the rough voice of a son-of-a-gun
  Of a watchman, "One o'clock," bawling.

Slowly and sadly we all walk'd down
  From his room in the uppermost story;
A rushlight we placed on the cold hearth-stone,
  And we left him alone in his glory.

Hos ego versiculos feci, tulit alter honores.—*Virgil.*
I wrote the verses, . . claimed them — he told stories.
                                    —*Thomas Ingoldsby.*

THE COUNTRY WEDDING.

UNKNOWN.   *From " Ritson's English Songs," 1783.*

WELL met, pretty nymph, says a jolly young swain,
To a lovely young shepherdess crossing the plain;
Why so much in haste? (Now the month it was May)
Shall I venture to ask you, fair maiden, which way?

Then strait to this question the nymph did reply,
With a smile on her look, and a leer on her eye,
I came from the village, and homeward I go;
And now, gentle shepherd, pray why would you know?

I hope, pretty maid, you wont take it amiss,
If I tell you the reason of asking you this;
I would see you safe home (the swain was in love),
Of such a companion if you would approve.

Your offer, kind shepherd, is civil I own,
But see no great danger in going alone;
Nor yet can I hinder, the road being free
For one as another, for you as for me.

No danger in going alone, it is true,
But yet a companion is pleasanter, too;
And if you could like (now the swain he took heart)
Such a sweetheart as me, we never would part.

O! that 's a long word, said the shepherdess then;
I 've often heard say, there 's no minding you men:
You 'll say and unsay, and you 'll flatter, 't is true;
Then leave a young maiden, the first thing you do.

O, judge not so harshly, the shepherd replied;
To prove what I say, I will make you my bride;
To-morrow the parson (well said, little swain)
Shall join both our hands, and make one of us twain.

Then what the nymph answer'd to this, is not said;
The very next morn, to be sure, they were wed.
Sing hey diddle, ho diddle, hey diddle down,
Now when shall we see such a wedding in town!

ON CHRISTMAS EVE.

ROBERT HERRICK,
1591–1674.

This poem, illustrative of old Christmas customs and superstitions, is selected from the "Hesperides" of Robert Herrick, first published in 1648.

COME bring with a noise,
My merry, merry boys,
The Christmas log to the firing;
While my good dame, she
Bids ye all be free,
And drink to your heart's desiring.

With the last year's brand [1]
Light the new block, and
For good success in his spending,
On your psalteries play,
That sweet luck may
Come while the log is a teending. [2]

Drink now the strong beer,
Cut the white loaf here,
The while the meat is a shredding
For the rare mince-pie,
And the plums standing by,
To fill the paste that 's a kneading.

---

[1] A portion of the log used to be preserved until the next year, with which to light the new block, and the omission to do so was deemed unlucky.

[2] Kindling.

4

TO THE GRASSHOPPER AND THE CRICKET.

LEIGH HUNT,
1784–1859.

Charles Cowden Clarke relates how during a visit paid by Keats and himself to Leigh Hunt, December 30, 1816, the host proposed to Keats " the challenge of writing then, there, and to time," a sonnet " On the Grasshopper and the Cricket." The following sonnet, and that on the opposite page, were the result of their friendly strife.

GREEN little vaulter in the sunny grass,
    Catching your heart up at the feel of June,
Sole voice that 's heard amidst the lazy noon,
When even the bees lag at the summoning brass;
And you, warm little housekeeper, who class
With those who think the candles come too soon,
Loving the fire, and with your tricksome tune
Nick the glad silent moments as they pass;
Oh, sweet and tiny cousins, that belong,
One to the fields, the other to the hearth,
Both have your sunshine; both though small are strong
At your clear hearts; and both were sent on earth
To sing in thoughtful ears this natural song:
In doors and out, summer and winter, Mirth.

ON THE GRASSHOPPER AND CRICKET.

JOHN KEATS,
1795-1821.

In this trial Keats won as to time; "but," Mr. Clarke continues, " with all the kind and gratifying things that were said to him, Keats protested to me, as we were afterwards walking home, that he preferred Hunt's treatment to his own."

THE poetry of earth is never dead:
  When all the birds are faint with the hot sun,
And hide in cooling trees, a voice will run
From hedge to hedge about the new-mown mead;
That is the grasshopper's—he takes the lead
In summer luxury,—he has never done
With his delights; for, when tired out with fun,
He rests at ease beneath some pleasant weed.
The poetry of earth is ceasing never:
On a lone winter evening, when the frost
Has wrought a silence, from the stove there shrills
The cricket's song, in warmth increasing ever,
And seems to one in drowsiness half lost,
The grasshopper's among some grassy hills.

AMINTOR'S WELL-A-DAY.

DR. H. H. HUGHES.   *From the Third Part of " Lawes's Ayres and Dialogues." 1658.*

CHLORIS, now thou art fled away,
    Amintor's sheep are gone astray,
And all the joy he took to see
His pretty lambs run after thee
    Is gone, is gone, and he alway
    Sings nothing now but well-a-day!

His oaten pipe, that in thy praise
Was wont to sing such roundelays,
Is thrown away, and not a swain
Dares pipe or sing within his plain,
    'T is death for any now to say
    One word to him but well-a-day!

The may-pole, where thy little feet
So roundly did in measure meet,
Is broken down, and no content
Comes near Amintor since you went,
    All that I ever heard him say
    Was Chloris, Chloris, well-a-day!

Upon those banks you used to tread,
He ever since hath laid his head,
And whisper'd there such pining woe,
As not a blade of grass will grow,—
    O Chloris, Chloris, come away,
    And hear Amintor's well-a-day!

LINES ON HEARING THE ORGAN.

C. S. CALVERLEY,
1831–1884.

From " Fly Leaves. Ninth Edition. London, 1883." Mr. Calverley was certainly one of the most successful and popular poets of an age in which few poets see many editions; and as the author of "Fly Leaves" was well known to all who liked mirth.

GRINDER, who serenely grindest
  At my door the Hundredth Psalm,
Till thou ultimately findest
  Pence in thy unwashen palm:

Grinder, jocund-hearted Grinder,
  Near whom Barbary's nimble son,
Poised with skill upon his hinder
  Paws, accepts the proffered bun:

Dearly do I love thy grinding;
  Joy to meet thee on thy road
Where thou prowlest through the blinding
  Dust with that stupendous load,

'Neath the baleful star of Sirius,
  When the postmen slowlier jog,
And the ox becomes delirious,
  And the muzzle decks the dog.

Tell me by what art thou bindest
  On thy feet those ancient shoon:
Tell me, Grinder, if thou grindest
  Always, always out of tune.

Tell me if, as thou art buckling
  On thy straps with eager claws,
Thou forcastest, inly chuckling,
  All the rage that thou wilt cause.

Tell me if at all thou mindest
  When folks flee, as if on wings,
From thee as at ease thou grindest:
  Tell me fifty thousand things.

Grinder, gentle-hearted Grinder!
  Ruffians who led evil lives,
Soothed by thy sweet strains, are kinder
  To their bullocks and their wives:

Children, when they see thy supple
  Form approach, are out like shots;
Half-a-bar sets several couple
  Waltzing in convenient spots;

Not with clumsy Jacks or Georges:
  Unprofaned by grasp of man,
Maidens speed those simple orgies,
  Betsy Jane with Betsy Ann.

As they love thee in St. Giles's
  Thou art loved in Grosvenor Square:
None of those engaging smiles is
  Unreciprocated there.

Often, ere yet thou hast hammer'd
  Through thy four delicious airs,
Coins are flung thee by enamour'd
  Housemaids upon area stairs:

E'en the ambrosial-whisker'd flunky
  Eyes thy boots and thine unkempt
Beard and melancholy monkey
  More in pity than contempt.

Far from England, in the sunny
  South, where Anio leaps in foam,
Thou wast rear'd, till lack of money
  Drew thee from thy vine-clad home:

And thy mate, the sinewy Jocko,
  From Brazil or Afric came,—
Land of simoom and sirocco,—
  And he seems extremely tame.

There he quaff'd the undefilèd
  Spring, or hung with apelike glee,
By his teeth or tail or eyelid,
  To the slippery mango-tree:

There he woo'd and won a dusky
  Bride, of instincts like his own;
Talk'd of love till he was husky
  In a tongue to us unknown:

Side by side 't was theirs to ravage
  The potato ground, or cut
Down the unsuspecting savage
  With the well-aim'd cocoa-nut:—

Till the miscreant stranger tore him
Screaming from his blue-faced fair;
And they flung strange raiment o'er him,
Raiment which he could not bear:

Sever'd from the pure embraces
Of his children and his spouse,
He must ride fantastic races
Mounted on reluctant sows:

But the heart of wistful Jocko
Still was with his ancient flame
In the nut-groves of Morocco;—
Or if not, it's all the same:

Grinder, winsome, grinsome Grinder!
They who see thee and whose soul
Melts not at thy charms, are blinder
Than a trebly-bandaged mole:

They to whom thy curt (yet clever)
Talk, thy music, and thine ape,
Seem not to be joys for ever,
Are but brutes in human shape.

'T is not that thy mien is stately,
'T is not that thy tones are soft;
'T is not that I care so greatly
For the same thing play'd so oft:

But I 've heard mankind abuse thee;
And perhaps it's rather strange,
But I thought that I would choose thee
For encomium, as a change.

THE SWEET NEGLECT.

BEN JONSON,
1574–1637.

This charming little madrigal (from Ben Jonson's "Silent Woman," act i. sc. 1, first acted in 1609) is in imitation of a Latin poem of Bonnefonius, beginning, " Semper munditias, semper Basilissa, decores," etc.

STILL to be neat, still to be drest,
    As you were going to a feast;
Still to be powder'd, still perfum'd:
Lady, it is to be presum'd,
Though art's hid causes be not found,
All is not sweet, all is not sound.

Give me a look, give me a face
That makes simplicity a grace;
Robes loosely flowing, hair as free:
Such sweet neglect more taketh me
Than all th' adulteries of art
That strike mine eyes, but not my heart.

TO THE LARK.

SIR JOHN DAVIES,
1570–1626.

*From " Hymns of Astræa, in Acrostic Verse,"
1599. Written in praise of Queen Elizabeth,
who is here addressed under the name of
Astræa.*

E ARLY, cheerful, mounting Lark!
Light's gentle usher! Morning's Clerk!
In merry notes delighting;
Stint awhile thy song, and hark,
And learn my new inditing!

Bear up this Hymn! to heaven, it bear!
Even up to heaven, and sing it there!
To heaven, each morning bear it!
Have it set to some sweet sphere,
And let the angels hear it!

Renowned ASTRÆA, that great name!
(Exceeding great in worth and fame,
Great worth hath so renowned it)
It is ASTRÆA's name I praise!
Now, then, sweet Lark! do thou it raise;
And in high heaven resound it!

A MESSAGE TO PHILLIS.

THOMAS HEYWOOD,
1575 ? – 1650 ?

*This song is extracted from Heywood's comedy
of " The Fair Maid of the Exchange," 1609.*

YE little birds that sit and sing
  Amidst the shady valleys,
And see how Phillis sweetly walks
  Within her garden alleys;
Go, pretty birds, about her bower,
Sing, pretty birds, she may not lower.
  Ah me! methinks I see her frown.
    Ye pretty wantons, warble.

Go tell her through your chirping bills,
  As you by me are bidden,
To her is only known my love,
  Which from the world is hidden:
Go, pretty birds, and tell her so,
See that your notes strain not too low;
  For still methinks I see her frown.
    Ye pretty wantons, warble.

Go tune your voices' harmony,
And sing I am her lover;
Strain loud and sweet, that every note
With sweet content may move her:
And she that hath the sweetest voice,
Tell her I will not change my choice;
Yet still methinks I see her frown.
Ye pretty wantons, warble.

O fly, make haste, see, see, she falls
Into a pretty slumber,
Sing round about her rosy bed,
That waking she may wonder;
Say to her, 't is her lover true,
That sendeth love to you, to you;
And when you have heard her kind reply,
Return with pleasant warblings.

IN PRAISE OF WINE.

UNKNOWN.

*From " Ritson's English Songs," 1783. This
song is, however, certainly older than 1754,
and as remodelled in our own days, " They
tell me I 've proved unkind to my Lass," is as
complete a statement of the superior advan-
tages of the flask as could be desired by its
most ardent advocate.*

THE women all tell me I 'm false to my lass,
    That I quit my poor Chloe, and stick to my glass;
But to you men of reason, my reasons I 'll own;
And if you don't like them, why—let them alone.

Although I have left her, the truth I 'll declare;
I believe she was good, and I 'm sure she was fair ;
But goodness and charms in a bumper I see,
That make it as good and as charming as she.

My Chloe had dimples and smiles, I must own ;
But though she could smile, yet in truth she could frown;
But tell me, ye lovers of liquor divine,
Did you e'er see a frown in a bumper of wine ?

Her lilies and roses were just in their prime ;
Yet lilies and roses are conquer'd by time :
But in wine, from its age such a benefit flows,
That we like it the better the older it grows.

They tell me my love would in time have been cloy'd,
And that beauty 's insipid when once 't is enjoy'd ;
But in wine I both time and enjoyment defy ;
For the longer I drink, the more thirsty am I.

Let murders, and battles, and history prove
The mischiefs that wait upon rivals in love ;
But in drinking, thank heaven, no rival contends,
For the more we love liquor, the more we are friends.

She, too, might have poison'd the joy of my life,
With nurses, and babies, and squalling, and strife
But my wine neither nurses nor babies can bring ;
And a big-bellied bottle 's a mighty good thing.

We shorten our days when with love we engage,
It brings on diseases and hastens old age ;
But wine from grim death can its votaries save,
And keep out t' other leg when there 's one in the grave.

Perhaps like her sex, ever false to their word,
She had left me to get an estate, or a lord ;
But my bumper (regarding nor title nor pelf)
Will stand by me when I can't stand by myself.

Then let my dear Chloe no longer complain ;
She 's rid of her lover, and I of my pain ;
For in wine, mighty wine, many comforts I spy ;
Should you doubt what I say, take a bumper and try.

A FICTION.

HOW CUPID MADE A NYMPH WOUND HERSELF
WITH HIS ARROWS.

FRANCIS DAVISON ?
1575 ?–1619 ?

This beautiful poem, which possesses a classical elegance hardly to be expected in the age of James I., is printed from " A Poetical Rhapsody" 1602, where it appeared signed " Anomos"; but it is attributed by Bishop Percy to Francis Davison.

IT chanced of late a shepherd's swain,
   That went to seek a strayèd sheep,
Within a thicket on the plain,
   Espied a dainty nymph asleep.

Her golden hair o'erspread her face,
   Her careless arms abroad were cast,
Her quiver had her pillow's place,
   Her breast lay bare to every blast.

The shepherd stood and gazed his fill;
   Nought durst he do, nought durst he say;
When chance, or else perhaps his will,
   Did guide the god of Love that way.

The crafty boy that sees her sleep,
  Whom if she waked, he durst not see,
Behind her closely seeks to creep,
  Before her nap should ended be.

There come, he steals her shafts away,
  And puts his own into their place;
Nor dares he any longer stay,
  But, ere she wakes, hies thence apace.

Scarce was he gone, when she awakes,
  And spies the shepherd standing by;
Her bended bow in haste she takes
  And at the simple swain lets fly.

Forth flew the shaft, and pierced his heart,
  That to the ground he fell with pain;
Yet up again forthwith did start,
  And to the nymph he ran amain.

Amazed to see so strange a sight,
  She shot, and shot, but all in vain;
The more his wounds, the more his might;
  Love yieldeth strength in midst of pain.

Her angry eyes are great with tears,
  She blames her hands, she blames her skill;
The bluntness of her shaft she fears,
  And try them on herself she will.

Take heed, sweet nymph! try not thy shaft;
  Each little touch will prick thy heart,
Alas! thou know'st not Cupid's craft;
  Revenge is joy, the end is smart.

5

Yet try she will, and pierce some bare;
  Her hands were glov'd, but next to hand
Was that fair breast, that breast so rare,
  That made the shepherd senseless stand.

That breast she pierced; and through that breast
  Love finds an entry to her heart:
.At feeling of this new-come guest,
  Lord! how the gentle nymph doth start!

She runs not now, she shoots no more,
  Away she throws both shafts and bow:
She seeks for that she shunn'd before,
  She thinks the shepherd's haste too slow.

Though mountains meet not, lovers may;
  What other lovers do, did they:
The god of Love sate on a tree,
  And laughed that pleasant sight to see.

AN OLD SONG OF AN OLD COURTIER
AND A NEW.

UNKNOWN.

Modified in succeeding reigns, the ballad of "The Queen [Elizabeth]'s Old Courtier and a New Courtier of the King [James]" has already known two hundred and fifty years' popularity. The earliest printed copy was probably issued by T. Symcocke, about 1626. The subject of this excellent old song is a comparison between the manners of the old gentry in the times of Elizabeth, and the modern refinements affected by their sons in the reigns of her successors.

WITH an old song made by an old ancient pate,
  Of an old worshipful gentleman who had a great estate;
Who kept an old house at a bountiful rate,
And an old porter to relieve the poor at his gate,
      Like an old Courtier of the Queen's.

With an old lady whose anger one good word assuages,
Who every quarter pays her old servants their wages,
Who never knew what belongs to coachman, footmen, and
      pages,
But kept twenty thrifty old fellows, with blue-coats and
      badges,
      Like an old Courtier of the Queen's.

With an old study fill'd full of learnèd books,
With an old reverend parson, you may judge him by his
    looks,
With an old buttery hatch worn quite off the old hooks,
And an old kitchen which maintains half a dozen old cooks;
                    Like an old Courtier of the Queen's.

With an old hall hung round about with guns, pikes, and bows,
With old swords and bucklers, which hath borne many shrewd
    blows,
And an old Frysadoe coat to cover his worship's trunk hose,
And a cup of old sherry to comfort his copper nose;
                    Like an old Courtier of the Queen's.

With an old fashion, when *Christmas* is come,
To call in his neighbours with bag-pipe and drum,
And good cheer enough to furnish every old room,
And old liquor able to make a cat speak, and a wise man dumb;
                    Like an old Courtier of the Queen's.

With an old hunts-man, a falconer, and a kennel of hounds;
Which never hunted nor hawked but in his own grounds,
Who like an old wise man kept himself within his own bounds,
And when he died gave every child a thousand old pounds;
                    Like an old Courtier of the Queen's.

But to his eldest son his house and land he assigned,
Charging him in his will to keep the same bountiful mind,
To be good to his servants, and to his neighbours kind,
But in th' ensuing ditty you shall hear how he was inclined;
                    Like a young Courtier of the King's.

PART SECOND.

Like a young gallant newly come to his land,
That keeps a brace of creatures at 's own command,
And takes up a thousand pounds upon 's own band,
And lieth drunk in a new tavern till he can neither go nor stand ;
     Like a young Courtier of the King's.

With a neat lady that is fresh and fair,
Who never knew what belonged to good housekeeping or care,
But buys several fans to play with the wanton air,
And seventeen or eighteen dressings of other women's hair ;
     Like a young Courtier of the King's.

With a new hall built where the old one stood,
Wherein is burned neither coal nor wood,
And a new shuffle-board-table where never meat stood,
Hung round with pictures which doth the poor little good,
     Like a young Courtier of the King's.

With a new study stuffed full of pamphlets and plays,
With a new chaplain that swears faster than he prays,
With a new buttery-hatch that opens once in four or five days,
With a new French cook to make kick-shawes and tayes ;
     Like a young Courtier of the King's.

With a new fashion when Christmas is come,
With a journey up to London we must be gone,
And leave nobody at home but our new porter John,
Who relieves the poor with a thump on the back with a stone ;
     Like a young Courtier of the King's.

With a gentleman-usher whose carriage is complete,
With a footman, a coachman, a page to carry meat,
With a waiting gentlewoman whose dressing is very neat,
Who when the master has dined gives the servants little meat;
                    Like a young Courtier of the King's.

With a new honour bought with his father's old gold,
That many of his father's old manors hath sold,
And this is the occasion that most men do hold,
That good housekeeping is now-a-days grown so cold;
                    Like a young Courtier of the King's.

THE FINE OLD ENGLISH GENTLEMAN.

Old songs have rarely, if ever, been modernized so successfully as the foregoing one of "The Queen's old Courtier," and "The Fine old English Gentleman," is no unworthy representative. Popular though it was, thirty or forty years ago, it is not easily met with now; on which account we hope we may be excused for adding it here.

I 'LL sing you a good old song, made by a good old pate,
Of a fine old English gentleman, who had an old estate,
And who kept up his old mansion, at a bountiful old rate;
With a good old porter to relieve the old poor at his gate,
   Like a fine old English gentleman, all of the olden time.

His hall so old was hung around with pikes, and guns, and bows,
And swords, and good old bucklers, that had stood against old
      foes;
'T was there " his worship " held his state in doublet and trunk
      hose,
And quaffed his cup of good old Sack to warm his good old
      nose;
         Like a fine old English gentleman, etc.

When winter's cold brought frost and snow, he opened house
    to all;
And though three score and ten his years, he featly led the
    ball;
Nor was the houseless wanderer e'er driven from his hall,
For, while he feasted all the great, he ne'er forgot the small;
                Like a fine old English gentleman, etc.

But time, though sweet, is strong in flight, and years roll swiftly
    by;
And autumn's falling leaves proclaimed the old man — he must
    die !
He laid him down right tranquilly, gave up life's latest sigh;
While a heavy stillness reign'd around, and tears dimm'd every
    eye.
                For this fine old English gentleman, etc.

Now surely this is better far than all the new parade
Of theatres and fancy balls, " At Home," and masquerade;
And much more economical, when all the bills are paid;
Then leave your new vagaries off, and take up the old trade
                Of a fine old English gentleman, etc.

OLDEN LOVE-MAKING.

NICHOLAS BRETON,
1542–1626?

Nicholas Breton was a writer of some fame in the reign of Elizabeth. He is mentioned with great respect by Meres in his second part of "Wit's Commonwealth," 1598; and is alluded to in Beaumont and Fletcher's "Scornful Lady," act ii.

IN time of yore, when shepherds dwelt
  Upon the mountain rocks;
And simple people never felt
  The pain of lovers' mocks;
But little birds would carry tales
  'Twixt Susan and her sweeting;
And all the dainty nightingales
  Did sing at lovers' meeting;
Then might you see what looks did pass
  Where shepherds did assemble;
And where the life of true love was
  When hearts could not dissemble.

Then yea and nay was thought an oath
  That was not to be doubted;
And when it came to faith and troth
  We were not to be flouted.
Then did they talk of curds and cream,
  Of butter, cheese, and milk;

There was no speech of sunny beam,
  Nor of the golden silk.   .
Then for a gift a row of pins,
  A purse, a pair of knives,
Was all the way that love begins,
  And so the shepherd wives.

But now we have so much ado,
  And are so sore aggrieved,
That when we go about to woo
  We cannot be believed.
Such choice of jewels, rings, and chains,
  That may but favour move;
And such intolerable pains
  Ere one can hit on love,
That if I still shall bide this life
  'Twixt love and deadly hate,
I will go learn the country life,
  Or leave the lover's state.

IN THE GLOAMING.

C. S. CALVERLEY,
1831–1884.

From "Fly Leaves. Ninth Edition. London, 1883."

I N the gloaming to be roaming, where the crested waves
are foaming,
  And the shy mermaidens combing locks that ripple to
  their feet;
When the gloaming is, I never made the ghost of an endeavour
To discover—but whatever were the hour, it would be sweet.

" To their feet," I say, for Leech's sketch indisputably teaches
  That the mermaids of our beaches do not end in ugly tails,
Nor have homes among the corals; but are shod with neat
  balmorals,
  An arrangement no one quarrels with, as many might with
  scales.

Sweet to roam beneath a shady cliff, of course with some
  young lady,
  Lalage, Neæra, Haidee, or Elaine, or Mary Ann:
Love, you dear delusive dream, you! Very sweet your victims
  deem you,
  When, heard only by the seamew, they talk all the stuff
  one can.

Sweet to haste a licensed lover, to Miss Pinkerton the glover,
   Having managed to discover what is dear Neæra's " size " :
P'raps to touch that wrist so slender, as your tiny gift you tender,
   And to read you 're no offender, in those laughing hazel eyes.

Then to hear her call you " Harry," when she makes you fetch
     and carry —
   O young men about to marry, what a blessed thing it is!
To be photographed — together — cased in pretty Russian
     leather —
   Hear her gravely doubting whether they have spoilt your
     honest phiz.

Then to bring your plighted fair one first a ring — a rich and
     rare one —
   Next a bracelet, if she 'll wear one, and a heap of things
     beside ;
And serenely bending o'er her, to inquire if it would bore her,
   To say when her own adorer may aspire to call her bride!

Then, the days of courtship over, with your WIFE to start for
     Dover
   Or Dieppe — and live in clover evermore, whate'er befalls :
For I 've read in many a novel that, unless they 've souls that
     grovel,
   Folks *prefer* in fact a hovel, to your dreary marble halls :

To sit, happy married lovers; Phyllis trifling with a plover's
   Egg, while Corydon uncovers with a grace the Sally Lunn,
Or dissects the lucky pheasant — that, I think, were passing
     pleasant ;
   As I sit alone at present, dreaming darkly of a Dun.

THE DUMB MAID.

UNKNOWN.

This merry ditty has continued to enjoy favour to the present time, lingering in many a quiet country nook, and adding point to innumerable sarcasms against the not " rara avis in terra" a Scolding Wife.—Our copy is from a black-letter ballad printed about 1678, and included in the Roxburghe Collection in the British Museum.

ALL you that pass along, give ear unto my song,
  Concerning a Youth that was young, young, young;
And a maiden fair, few with her might compare,
  But alack, and alas ! she was dumb, dumb, dumb.

She was beauteous, fresh, and gay, like the pleasant flowers in
    May,
  And her cheeks were as round as a plum, plum, plum,
She was neat in every part, and she stole away his heart;
  But alack, and alas ! she was dumb, dumb, dumb.

At length this Country Blade wedded this pretty Maid,
  And he kindly conducted her home, home, home.
Thus in her beauty bright lay all his whole delight;
  But alack, and alas ! she was dumb, dumb, dumb.

Now will I plainly show what work this maid could do,
  Which a pattern may be for girls young, young, young.
O she, both day and night, in working took delight,
  But alack, and alas! she was dumb, dumb, dumb.

She could brew and she could bake, she could wash, wring,
    and shake,
  She could sweep the house with a broom, broom, broom;
She could knit, and sew, and spin, and do any such like thing,
  But alack, and alas! she was dumb, dumb, dumb.

But at last this man did go, the doctor's skill to know,
  Saying, " Sir, can you cure a woman of the dumb, dumb,
    dumb ? "
" O it is the easiest part that belongs unto my art,
  For to cure any woman of the *dumb, dumb, dumb.*"

To the doctor he did her bring, and he cut her chattering-string,
  And he quickly set her tongue on the run, run, run.
In the morning she did rise, and she filled his house with cries,
  And she rattled in his ears *like a drum, drum, drum.*

To the doctor he did go, with his heart well filled with woe,
  Crying, " Doctor, I am certainly undone, done, done!
Now she 's turned a scolding wife, and I 'm weary of my life,
  Nor I cannot make her *hold her tongue, tongue, tongue !* "

The doctor thus did say, " When she went from me away,
  She was perfectly cured of the dumb, dumb, dumb;
But it 's beyond the art of man, let him do the best he can,
  For to make a scolding woman *hold her tongue, tongue,
    tongue.*"

"THE HUNT IS UP."

UNCERTAIN.

*Among the favorites of Henry VIII., Putten-
ham, in his " Arte of English Poesie," 1589,
notices " one Gray, for making certain merry
ballades, whereof one chiefly was, ' The hunte
is up, the hunte is up.' " It may be that the
following song is the very one written by
Gray, since "Harry our King" is twice mentioned in it. Any song intended to arouse in
the morning—even a love song—was for-
merly called a " hunt 's up."*

THE hunt is up, the hunt is up,
   And it is well nigh day;
And Harry our King is gone hunting,
   To bring his deer to bay.

The east is bright with morning light,
   And darkness it is fled,
And the merie horne wakes up the morne
   To leave his idle bed.

Behold the skyes with golden dyes
   Are glowing all around,
The grasse is greene, and so are the treene
   All laughing at the sound.

The horses snort to be at the sport,
  The dogges are running free,
The woddes rejoyce at the mery noise
  Of hey tantara tee ree!

The sunne is glad to see us clad
  All in our lustie greene,
And smiles in the skye as he riseth hye,
  To see and to be seene.

Awake, all men, I say agen,
  Be mery as you maye,
For Harry our King is gone hunting,
  To bring his deere to baye.

ON AN OLD MUFF.

FREDERICK LOCKER,
Born 1821.

*This poem by Mr. Locker was first published in
1865, and is taken from "London Lyrics"—
(latest edition, 1876).*

TIME has a magic wand!
    What is this meets my hand,
Moth-eaten, mouldy, and
    Covered with fluff?
Faded, and stiff, and scant;
Can it be? no, it can't —
Yes,— I declare 't is Aunt
    Prudence's Muff!

Years ago — twenty-three!
Old Uncle Barnaby
Gave it to Aunty P.—
    Laughing and teasing —
" Pru., of the breezy curls,
Whisper these solemn churls,
*What holds a pretty girl's
    Hand without squeezing?* "

6

Uncle was then a lad
Gay, but, I grieve to add,
Sinful : if smoking bad
    Baccy 's a vice :
Glossy was then this mink
Muff, lined with pretty pink
Satin, which maidens think
    "Awfully nice ! "

I see, in retrospect,
Aunt, in her best bedecked,
Gliding, with mien erect,
    Gravely to Meeting :
Psalm-book, and kerchief new,
Peeped from the muff of Pru.—
Young men — and pious, too —
    Giving her greeting.

Pure was the life she led
Then — from this Muff, 't is said,
Tracts she distributed :—
    Scapegraces many,
Seeing the grace they lacked,
Followed her — one, in fact,
Asked for — and got his tract
    Oftener than any.

Love has a potent spell !
Soon this bold ne'er-do-well,
Aunt's sweet susceptible
    Heart undermining,

Slipped, so the scandal runs,
Notes in the pretty nun's
Muff — triple-cornered ones —
    Pink as its lining !

Worse even, soon the jade,
Fled (to oblige her blade !)
Whilst her friends thought that they 'd
    Locked her up tightly :
After such shocking games
Aunt is of wedded dames
Gayest — and now her name 's
    Mrs. Golightly.

In female conduct flaw
Sadder I never·saw,
Still I 've faith in the law
    Of compensation.
Once Uncle went astray —
Smoked, joked, and swore away —
Sworn by he 's now, by a
    Large congregation !

Changed is the Child of Sin,
Now he 's (he once was thin)
Grave, with a double chin, —
    Blest be his fat form !
Changed is the garb he wore, —
Preacher was never more
Prized than is Uncle for
    Pulpit or platform.

If all 's as best befits
Mortals of slender wits,
Then beg this Muff, and its
    Fair owner, pardon:
All 's for the best,—indeed,
Such is *my* simple creed,—
Still I must go and weed
    Hard in my garden.

KING OBERON'S FEAST.

ROBERT HERRICK,
1591-1674.

This poem was printed in "A Description of the King and Queen of Fairies; their habit, fare, their abode, pomp, and state. Being very delightful to the sense, and full of mirth." 1635. The "Feast," the only one, of the several poems contained in this book, which can be assigned with absolute certainty to Herrick, was, it is believed, the poet's earliest appearance in print.

A LITTLE mushroom-table spread,
    After short prayers, they set on bread;
A moon-parch'd grain of purest wheat,
With some small glitt'ring grit, to eat
His choice bits with; then in a trice
They make a feast less great than nice.
But all this while his eye is served,
We must not think his ear was starved:
But that there was in place to stir
His spleen, the chirping Grasshopper;
The merry Cricket, puling Fly,
The piping Gnat for minstrelsy.
And now, we must imagine first,
The Elves present to quench his thirst
A pure seed-pearl of infant dew,
Brought and besweeten'd in a blue

And pregnant violet; which done,
His kitling[1] eyes begin to run
Quite through the table, where he spies
The horns of papery butterflies:
Of which he eats, and tastes a little
Of what we call the cuckoo-spittle.[2]
A little fuz-ball[3] pudding stands
By, yet not blessed by his hands,
That was too coarse; but then forthwith
He ventures boldly on the pith
Of sugared rush, and eats the sag
And well bestrutted[4] bee's sweet bag:
Gladding[5] his palate with some store
Of Emmet's[6] eggs: what would he more?
But beards of mice, a newt's[7] stewed thigh,
A bloated ear-wig, and a fly;
With the red-capped worm, that 's shut
Within the concave of a nut,
Brown as his tooth. A little moth,
Late fatten'd in a piece of cloth:
With withered cherries; mandrakes' ears;
Moles' eyes; to these, the slain-stag's tears;
The unctuous dewlaps of a snail;

---

[1] Eyes like kittens (green).
[2] The white froth which encloses the larva of the cicàda spumarià.
[3] Puff-balls, or fungus.
[4] "Sag" means "heavy," so as to hang down. The meaning here is —
He eats the pith of the sweet "Rush" and the bag of the bee. The flight
of a bee to her hive is thus graphically described — i. e., "sagged down" with
the weight of her spoils. The word bestrutted is equally descriptive of the
laden bee labouring along, with legs stuck out, like "struts," or props.
[5] Pleasing, i. e., tickling.   [6] Ant.   [7] Small lizard.

The broke-heart of a nightingale
O'ercome in musick; with a wine,
Ne'er ravish'd from the flatt'ring vine,
But gently pressed from the soft side
Of the most sweet and dainty bride,
Brought in a dainty daisy, which
He fully quaffs up to bewitch
His blood to height; this done, commended
Grace by his Priest; *the feast is ended.*

A CHRISTMAS SONG.

UNKNOWN.

The old almanacks occasionally contained carols. The following is from "Poor Robin's Almanack" for 1695.

N OW thrice welcome Christmas,
　　Which brings us good cheer,
Minc'd pies and plum-porridge,
　　Good ale and strong beer ;
With pig, goose, and capon,
　　The best that can be,
So well doth the weather
　　And our stomachs agree.

Observe how the chimnies
　　Do smoke all about,
The cooks are providing
　　For dinner, no doubt ;
But those on whose tables
　　No victuals appear,
O may they keep Lent
　　All the rest of the year !

With holly and ivy
  So green and so gay;
We deck up our houses
  As fresh as the day,
With bays and rosemary
  And laurel complete,
And every one now
  Is a king in conceit.

TO DAFFODILS.

Robert Herrick,
1591–1674.

Surely there is no flower-poem at once so weighty and so sweet, so lovely and also impressive, so consummate in its art and enduring in its charm as this one of Herrick's.

Fair Daffodils, we weep to see
   You haste away so soon:
As yet the early-rising sun
   Has not attained his noon.
     Stay, stay
   Until the hasting day
      Has run
   But to the even-song;
And, having prayed together, we
   Will go with you along.

We have short time to stay, as you,
   We have as short a Spring;
As quick a growth to meet decay,
   As you or any thing.
     We die,
   As your hours do, and dry
      Away,
   Like to the summer's rain;
Or as the pearls of morning's dew,
   Ne'er to be found again.

THE CHILD MUSICIAN.

AUSTIN DOBSON,
Born 1840.

From " Vignettes in Rhyme," 1873.

H E had played for his lordship's levee,
       He had played for her ladyship's whim,
Till the poor little head was heavy,
    And the poor little brain would swim.

And the face grew peaked and eerie,
    And the large eyes strange and bright,
And they said — too late—" He is weary!
    He shall rest for, at least, To-night! "

But at dawn, when the birds were waking,
    As they watched in the silent room,
With the sound of a strained cord breaking,
    A something snapped in the gloom.

'T was a string of his violoncello,
    And they heard him stir in his bed :—
" Make room for a tired little fellow,
    Kind God! " — was the last that he said.

THE BITER BIT.

A PARODY.

"The Biter Bit," from the "Bon Gaultier Ballads," 1845, by Theodore Martin and Professor Aytoun, is a kind of burlesque continuation of the "May Queen," the tender pathos of the original being turned into cynical indifference, whilst preserving a great similarity of style and versification.

THE sun is in the sky, mother, the flowers are springing fair,
And the melody of woodland birds is stirring in the air;
The river, smiling to the sky, glides onward to the sea,
And happiness is everywhere, oh mother, but with me!

They are going to the church, mother,— I hear the marriage bell;
It rises o'er the upland,—it haunts me like a knell;
He leads her on his arm, mother, he cheers her faltering step,
And she clings closely to his side, she does, the demirep!

They are crossing by the stile, mother, where we so oft have stood,—
The stile beside the thorn at the corner of the wood;
The boughs, that oft have echoed back the words that won my ear,
Now bend their blossoms o'er him as he leads his bridal fere.

He will pass beside the stream, mother, where first my hand
    he pressed,
By the meadow where, with quivering lip, his passion he
    confessed;
And down the hedgerows where we 've strayed again and
    yet again;
Yet he will not think of me, mother, his broken-hearted Jane!

He said that I was proud, mother, he said I looked for gold;
He said I did not love him,— that my words were few and
    cold;
He said I kept him off and on, in hopes of higher game,—
And it may be that I did, mother; but who has n't done the
    same?

I did not know my heart, mother,— I know it now too late;
I thought that I without a pang could wed some nobler mate;
But no nobler suitor sought me,— and he has gone elsewhere,
And my heart is gone, and I am left to wither in despair.

You may lay me in my bed, mother, my head is throbbing sore;
And, mother, prithee let the sheets be duly aired before;
And, if you would do pleasure to your poor desponding child,
Draw me a pot of beer, mother, and, mother, draw it mild!

THE JOLLY BACCHANAL.

UNKNOWN.   *From " Walsh's British Musical Miscellany."*

LET 'S tope and be merry, be jolly and cherry,
   Since here is good wine, good wine ;
Let 's laugh at the fools that live by dull rules,
  And at us good fellows repine,
     And at us good fellows repine.

Here, here, are delights to amuse the dull nights,
  And equal a man with a god ;
To enliven the clay, drive all care away,
  Without which a man 's but a clod.

Then let us be willing to spend t' other shilling,
  Since money we know is but dirt;
It suits no design like paying for wine,
  T' other bottle will do us no hurt.

UNFADING BEAUTY.

THOMAS CAREW,
1589-1639.

This beautiful little sonnet is reprinted from a small volume entitled " Poems by Thomas Carew, Esq., one of the gentlemen of the privie-chamber, and sewer in ordinary to his majesty. London, 1640." We have omitted the third stanza as not being of equal merit.

H E, that loves a rosy cheek,
   Or a coral lip admires,
Or from star-like eyes doth seek
   Fuel to maintain his fires,
As old time makes these decay,
So his flames must waste away.

But a smooth and steadfast mind,
   Gentle thoughts and calm desires,
Hearts with equal love combined,
   Kindle never-dying fires.
Where these are not, I despise
Lovely cheeks, or lips, or eyes.

TO CHLOE JEALOUS.

Matthew Prior,
1664–1721.

D EAR Chloe, how blubber'd is that pretty face!
Thy cheek all on fire and thy hair all uncurl'd!
Prithee quit this caprice, and (as old Falstaff says)
Let us e'en talk a little like folks of this world.

How canst thou presume thou hast leave to destroy
The beauties which Venus but lent to thy keeping?
Those looks were design'd to inspire love and joy:
More ord'nary eyes may serve people for weeping.

To be vexed at a trifle or two that I writ,
Your judgment at once, and my passion you wrong:
You take that for fact which will scarce be found wit:
Odslife! must one swear to the truth of a song?

What I speak, my fair Chloe, and what I write shows
The diff'rence there is betwixt nature and art:
I court others in verse; but I love thee in prose:
And they have my whimsies, but thou hast my heart.

The God of us verse men (you know child) the Sun,
　How after his journeys he sets up his rest :
If at morning o'er earth 't is his fancy to run ;
　At night he reclines on his Thetis's breast.

So when I am wearied with wand'ring all day ;
　To thee my delight in the evening I come :
No matter what beauties I saw in my way :
　They were but my visits ; but thou art my home.

Then finish, dear Chloe, this pastoral war ;
　And let us like Horace and Lydia agree :
For thou art a girl as much brighter than her,
　As he was a poet sublimer than me.

THE CONSTITUTION AND THE GUERRIERE.

UNKNOWN.

The naval battle which this song celebrates was fought on August 19th, 1812, between the American frigate Constitution, commanded by Captain Isaac Hull, and his Britannic Majesty's frigate Guerrière, Captain Dacres; —after a severe and bloody engagement lasting only half an hour the latter surrendered.

I OFTEN have been told,
  That the British seamen bold
Could beat the tars of France, neat and handy, O;
  But they never found their match,
  Till the Yankees did them catch—
For the Yankee tars for fighting are the dandy, O!

  O, the Guerriere so bold,
  On the foaming ocean roll'd,
Commanded by Dacres the grandee, O!
  With as choice a British crew
  As a rammer ever drew,
They could beat the Frenchmen two to one, so handy, O!

  When this frigate hove in view;
  "O," said Dacres to his crew,
"Prepare ye for action and be handy, O:
  On the weather-gauge we'll get her,
  And to make the men fight better
We will give to them gunpowder and good brandy, O."

Now this boasting Briton cries,
" Make that Yankee ship your prize,
You can in thirty minutes do it handy, O :
Or in twenty-five I 'm sure ;
If you 'll do it in a score,
I 'll give you a double share of good brandy, O.

" When prisoners we 've made them,
With switchel we will treat them ;
We 'll welcome them with Yankee Doodle Dandy, O ":
O, the British balls flew hot,
But the Yankees answered not,
Until they got a distance that was handy, O.

" O," cries Hull unto his crew,
" We will try what we can do :
If we beat those boasting Britons we 're the dandy, O."
The first broadside we pour'd
Brought the mizzen by the board,
Which doused the royal ensign quite handy, O.

O, Dacres he did sigh,
And to his officers did cry,
" O! I did n't think the Yankees were so handy, O."
The second told so well,
That the fore and main-mast fell,
That made this lofty frigate look quite dandy, O.

" O !" said Dacres, " we 're undone":
So he fires a lee gun,
And the drummers struck up Yankee Doodle Dandy, O.
When Dacres came on board,
To deliver up his sword
He was loth to part with it, it look'd so handy, O.

"You may keep it," says brave Hull;
"What makes you look so dull?
Cheer up and take a glass of good brandy, O."
O, Britons now be still,
Since we 've hook'd you in the gill:
Don't boast upon your Dacres, the grandee, O.

Come, fill your glasses full,
And we 'll drink to Captain Hull,
And so merrily we 'll push about the brandy, O.
John Bull may toast his fill,
Let the world say what it will,
But the Yankee boys for fighting are the dandy, O.

"COME, SHEPHERDS, DECK YOUR HEADS."

UNKNOWN.

This is one of the songs mentioned by genial old Izaak Walton in "The Complete Angler," 1653.— MILKWOMAN: *"What song was it, I pray? was it 'Come, shepherds, deck your heads'; or, 'As, at noon Dulcina rested'; or, 'Phillida flouts me'; or, 'Chevy Chace'; or, 'Johnny Armstrong'; or, 'Troy Town'?"*

COME, Shepherds, deck your heads
 No more with bays but willows;
Forsake your downy beds,
 And make the downs your pillows:
And mourn with me, since crossed
 As never yet was no man,
For shepherd never lost
 So plain a dealing woman.

All ye forsaken wooers,
 That ever care oppressed,
And all you lusty dooers,
 That ever love distressed,
That losses can condole,
 And all together summon;
Oh! mourn for the poor soul
 Of my plain-dealing woman.

Fair Venus made her chaste,
    And Ceres beauty gave her;
Pan wept when she was lost,
    The Satyis strove to have her;
Yet seem'd she to their view
    So coy, so nice, that no man
Could judge, but he that knew
    My own plain-dealing woman.

At all her pretty parts
    I ne'er enough can wonder;
She overcame all hearts,
    Yet she all hearts came under;
Her inward mind was sweet,
    Good tempers ever common;
Shepherd shall never meet
    So plain a dealing woman.

THE BROWN JUG.

REV. FRANCIS FAWKES,
1721–1777.

It is somewhat remarkable that the two best drinking songs in our language were both by clergymen; the following by Rev. Francis Fawkes, and that on page 18 by John Still, bishop of Bath and Wells; 1543–1607.

DEAR TOM, this brown jug, that now foams with mild ale,
  (In which I will drink to sweet Nan of the Vale)
Was once Toby Fillpot, a thirsty old soul
As e'er drank a bottle or fathomed a bowl;
In boosing about 't was his praise to excel,
And among jolly topers he bore off the bell.

It chanced, as in dog-days he sat at his ease,
In his flower-woven arbour, as gay as you please,
With a friend and a pipe, puffing sorrows away,
And with honest old Stingo was soaking his clay,
His breath-doors of life on a sudden were shut,
And he died full as big as a Dorchester butt.

His body when long in the ground it had lain,
And time into clay had resolved it again,
A potter found out in its covert so snug,
And with part of fat Toby he formed this brown jug;
Now sacred to friendship, to mirth, and mild ale,
So here 's to my lovely sweet Nan of the Vale.

THE LOVE PARTING.

MICHAEL DRAYTON,
1563–1631.

" From Anacreon down to Moore," says Henry Reed, speaking of this sonnet, " I know of no lines on the old subject of lovers' quarrels distinguished for equal tenderness of sentiment and richness of fancy."

SINCE there 's no help, come let us kiss and part,—
   Nay, I have done, you get no more of me;
And I am glad, yea, glad with all my heart,
   That thus so cleanly I myself can free;
Shake hands forever, cancel all our vows,
   And when we meet at any time again,
Be it not seen in either of our brows
   That we one jot of former love retain.
Now at the last gasp of Love's latest breath,
   When, his pulse failing, Passion speechless lies,
When Faith is kneeling by his bed of death,
   And Innocence is closing up his eyes,—
Now if thou would'st, when all have given him over,
From death to life thou might'st him yet recover!

LOVE'S ANNIVERSARY.

TO THE SUN.

WILLIAM HABINGTON,
1605–1645.

From "Castara: The Third Edition. Corrected and augmented. 1640." This work, "one of the most elegant monuments ever raised by genius to conjugal affection," says Mrs. Jameson, was first published in 1634.

THOU art returned, great light, to that blest hour
In which I first by marriage, sacred power,
Joined with *Castara* heart: and as the same
Thy lustre is, as then, so is our flame;
Which had increased, but that by love's decree
'T was such at first it ne'er could greater be.
But tell me, glorious lamp, in thy survey
Of things below thee, what did not decay
By age to weakness? I since that have seen
The rose bud forth and fade, the tree grow green
And wither, and the beauty of the field
With winter wrinkled. Even thyself doth yield
Something to time, and to thy grave fall nigher;—
But virtuous love is one sweet endless fire.

"PHYLLIDA, THAT LOVED TO DREAM."

JOHN GAY,
1688–1732.

PHYLLIDA, that loved to dream
  In the grove, or by the stream;
    Sigh'd on velvet pillow.
What, alas! should fill her head,
But a fountain, or a mead,
    Water and a willow?

Love in cities never dwells,
He delights in rural cells
    Which sweet woodbine covers.
What are your assemblies then?
There 't is true, we see more men;
    But much fewer lovers.

O, how changed the prospect grows!
Flocks and herds to fops and beaux,
    Coxcombs without number!
Moon and stars that shone so bright;
To the torch and waxen light,
    And whole nights at ombre.[1]

---

[1] A fashionable game of the period.

Pleasant as it is to hear
Scandal tickling in our ear,
  E'en of our own mothers;
In the chit-chat of the day
To us is paid, when we 're away,
  What we lent to others.

Though the favourite Toast I reign,
Wine, they say, that prompts the vain,
  Heightens defamation.
Must I live 'twixt spite and fear,
Every day grow handsomer,
  And lose my reputation ?

·Thus the fair to sighs gave way,
Her empty purse beside her lay.
  Nymph, ah! cease thy sorrow. -
Though curst Fortune frown to-night,
This odious town can give delight,
  If you win to-morrow.

SONG OF IN-THE-WATER.

H. CHOLMONDELEY— PENNELL.

Longfellow's "Song of Hiawatha" certainly invites parody, and its easy metre is readily caught up by any one having an ordinarily good ear, and knack of versification. The following imitation of it is from "Puck on Pegasus." London, 1868.

WHEN the summer night descended,
   Sleepy on the White-witch water,
Came a lithe and lovely maiden,
Gazing on the silent water—
Gazing on the gleaming river—
With her azure eyes and tender,—
On the river glancing forward,
Till the am'rous wave sprang upward,
Upward from his reedy hollow,
With the lily in his bosom,
With his crown of water-lilies—
Curling ev'ry dimpled ripple
As he sprang into the starlight,
As he clasped her charmed reflection
Glowing to his crystal bosom —
As he whispered, " Fairest, fairest,
Rest upon this crystal bosom ! "

And she straightway did according :—

Down into the water stept she,
Down into the wavering river,
Like a red deer in the sunset—
Like a ripe leaf in the Autumn:
From her lips, as rose-buds snow-filled,
Came a soft and dreamy murmur,
Softer than the breath of summer,
   Softer than the murm'ring river,
   Than the cooing of Cushawa,—
Sighs that melted as the snows melt,
   Silently and sweetly melted;
Sounds that mingled with the crisping
   Foam upon the billows resting:

Yet she spoke not, only murmured.

   From the forest shade primeval,
Piggey-Wiggey looked out at her;
   He, the very Youthful Porker—
   He, the Everlasting Grunter—
Gazed upon her there, and wondered!
   With his nose out, Rokey-pokey—
   And his tail up, Curley-wurley,
Wondered what on earth the joke was,
Wondered what the girl was up to,
What the deuce her little game was,
Why she did n't squeak and grunt more!

And she floated down the river,
Like a water-proof Ophelia,
FOR HER CRINOLINE SUSTAINED HER.

GOD REST YOU, MERRY GENTLEMEN.

UNKNOWN.

There is no carol, perhaps, so universally known as this. Many who have heard no other are familiar with this, and speak of it as The Christmas Carol. While there are several variations in the different copies of this carol, the version here printed seems the most generally received, and is perhaps the most genuine.

GOD rest you, merry gentlemen,
  Let nothing you dismay,
Remember Christ, our Saviour,
  Was born on Christmas-day;
To save us all from Satan's power,
  When we were gone astray.
    O tidings of comfort and joy,
    For Jesus Christ, our Saviour, was
    Born of Christmas-day.

In Bethlehem, in Jewry,
  This blessed babe was born,
And laid within a manger
  Upon this blessed morn;
The which His mother Mary
  Did nothing take in scorn.
    O tidings, etc.

From God, our Heavenly Father,
　A blessed Angel came,
And unto certain shepherds
　Brought tidings of the same ;
That there was born in Bethlehem
　The Son of God by name.
　　O tidings, etc.

" Fear not," then said the Angel,
　" Let nothing you affright,
For there is born in Bethlehem
　Of a pure Virgin bright,
One able to advance you,
　And throw down Satan quite."
　　O tidings, etc.

The shepherds, at those tidings,
　Rejoiced much in mind,
And left their flocks a-feeding
　In tempest, storm, and wind,
And straightway went to Bethlehem
　The Son of God to find.
　　O tidings, etc.

But when they came to Bethlehem,
　Where as this Infant lay,
They found Him in a manger,
　Where oxen feed on hay,
His mother Mary kneeling down,
　Unto the Lord did pray.
　　O tidings, etc.

With sudden joy and gladness
  The shepherds were beguiled,
To see the Babe of Israel,
  Before His mother mild.
O then with joy and cheerfulness
  Rejoice, each mother's child.
    O tidings, etc.

Now to the Lord sing praises,
  All you within this place,
And with true love and brotherhood
  Each other now embrace,
This holy tide of Christmas
  All others doth deface.
    O tidings, etc.

God bless the ruler of this house,
  And send him long to reign,
And many a merry Christmas
  May he live to see again
Among his friends and kindred
  That live both far and near;
  And God send you a happy New Year.

DRINKING SONG.

UNKNOWN.   *From " Ritson's English Songs," 1783.*

HAD Neptune, when first he took charge of the sea,
Been as wise, or at least been as merry as we,
He 'd have thought better on 't, and, instead of his brine,
Would have filled the vast ocean with generous wine.

What trafficking, then, would have been on the main,
For the sake of good liquor, as well as for gain!
No fear then of tempest, or danger of sinking;
The fishes ne'er drown that are always a-drinking.

The hot, thirsty Sun then would drive with more haste,
Secure in the evening of such a repast;
And when he 'd got tipsy would have taken his nap,
With double the pleasure in Thetis's lap.

By the force of his rays, and thus heated with wine,
Consider how gloriously Phœbus would shine;
What vast exhalations he 'd draw up on high,
To relieve the poor earth as it wanted supply.

8

How happy us mortals when bless'd with such rain,
To fill all our vessels, and fill them again!
Nay, even the beggar that has ne'er a dish,
Might jump in the river and drink like a fish.

What mirth and contentment in every one's brow,
Hob as great as a prince dancing after the plow!
The birds in the air, as they play on the wing,
Although they but sip, would eternally sing.

The stars, who I think don't to drinking incline,
Would frisk and rejoice at the fume of the wine;
And, merrily twinkling, would soon let us know
That they were as happy as mortals below.

Had this been the case, what had we then enjoy'd,
Our spirits still rising, our fancy ne'er cloy'd!
A plague, then, on Neptune, when 't was in his power,
To slip, like a fool, such a fortunate hour.

LITTLE BO-PEEP.

H. CHOLMONDELEY-PENNELL.   *The following is from a little volume of poems by Mr. Cholmondeley-Pennell, entitled "From Grave to Gay." London, 1884.*

" LITTLE BO-PEEP has lost her sheep,"
And some one or other 's lost little Bo-peep —
Or she 'd never be wand'ring at twelve o'clock
With a golden crook and a velvet frock,
In a diamond necklace, in such a rout, —
In diamond buckles and high heel'd shoes
(And a dainty wee foot in them, too, if you choose,
And an ankle a sculptor might rave about . . . .)
But I think she 's a little witch, you know,
With her broomstick-crook and her high-heel'd shoe
And the mischievous fun that flashes thro'
The wreaths of her amber hair—don't you ?
No wonder the flock follows little Bo-peep, —
Such a shepherd would turn all the world into sheep,
To trot at her heels and look up in the face
Of their pastor for—goodness knows what, say for grace ? —
Her face that recalls in its reds and its blues,
And its setting of gold, " Esmeralda " by Greuze. . . . .

There you 've Little Bo-peep, dress, diamonds, and all,
As I met her last night at the Fancy Ball.

"THERE IS A LIGHT."

R. D. YOUNG.

Mr. Young is a well-known merchant in New York City, whose business duties seldom permit him to drop into poetry. His Muse in this instance was doubtless inspired by the excellence of the subject.

THERE is a Light whose brightness vies
   With any planet in the skies;
That shines with kindlier lustre, far,
Than Venus in her silvery car;
For while this orb but coldly gleams,—
Ne'er shining, save with borrowed beams,
That Light, Promethean, warmly glows,—
Man's blessing in a world of woes!
More useful, often, is that Light,
Than Phœbus' ardent rays, so bright;
And while this sounds like fiction vain,
Let me its truthfulness maintain:—
The sun departs at close of day
And leaves behind no lingering ray,
Ah! then the skeptic well may guess
The "Astral's" greater usefulness!

Blest "Astral" oil! thy flood of light
Dispels the gloom of blackest night;
In peaceful homes, where love is queen,
How prized thy merits, bright, serene!

The old and young of every clime,
Around the hearth at even-time,
Both rich and poor, engaged howe'er,
Thy great beneficence declare.
Thy motto stands, in letters bright,
SAFETY, ECONOMY, DELIGHT!
No dread explosion dims thy fame,
No horrid smell infests thy name;
Health, weal and pleasure all attend,
And in thy presence hap'ly blend.

Then let us, e'er another e'en,
Discard both Gas and Kerosene,
And free our minds from all the care
They force us constantly to bear.
Their danger, trouble, and expense
Must surely drive them quickly hence,
And yield before the truth and might
Of Pratt's celestial "Astral" Light.

TABLE OF FIRST LINES.

 RATT'S ASTRAL OIL.

In a circular issued June 30th, 1882, by the New-York State Board of Health, there appears the astounding statement, "It is estimated that upwards of thirty thousand lives have been destroyed by the explosive qualities of petroleum." The introduction of PRATT'S ASTRAL OIL was the first practical check given to this wholesale destruction of life. Fifteen years ago, all burning oils made from petroleum were so unsafe that there was danger of their sale being prohibited by legislation. The demand was for a good illuminating oil that could be relied on as absolutely safe. After a long series of experiments, conducted at a large expense, we discovered a way to meet this public want.

This was the origin of the celebrated PRATT'S ASTRAL OIL, the first safe and reliable illuminating oil ever made; and although many millions of gallons have annually been sold since its introduction, no person has ever suffered by an accident from its use, nor has any Insurance Company paid a dollar for loss occasioned by it. It was originally sold at 60 cents per gallon, but by the improved processes of manufacture, necessitated by the largely increasing demand, we are enabled now to furnish it at a price within the means of the poorest family. Why, then, should any risk be taken in the choice of a burning oil, when PRATT'S ASTRAL OIL can be obtained for so small a cost?

RATT'S GASOLENE.

There is assuredly no better method of illumination for suburban residences, hotels, mills, and other large buildings than by means of Gas Machines. A most excellent and reliable quality of Gas can thus be obtained at a cost varying from about 75 cents to a little over $1.00 for light fully equal to 1000 feet of Coal Gas, or less than one-half the price usually charged for that article. No trouble attaches to their use, as most of them are automatic in their operation. Of these Machines, there are several varieties, differing both in their construction and operation, and possessing, of course, varying degrees of merit. Our acquaintance with the respective qualifications of each and our long familiarity with the subject may enable us to suggest the one best adapted for any required purpose, should any of our readers contemplate purchasing one.

We accordingly invite correspondence on this subject, and shall be pleased at all times to furnish full information about Gas Machines and all matters pertaining to the question of Gasolene Gas.

GASOLENE.—Nothing is so essential to the satisfactory and successful operation of Gas Machines as good Gasolene. Fluid of inferior quality is often offered for sale that is positively injurious to Gas Machines, and consumers will save themselves much trouble and expense by purchasing only a well-known and reliable article, and from responsible parties.—The best goods are invariably the cheapest in the end, and especially is this true of Gasolene. Good Gasolene cannot — like Kerosene Oil — be obtained from every dealer or even from every manufacturer.

Where consumers are unable to secure Pratt's Patent Prepared Gasolene from their present source of supply, if they will send their orders direct to us, they will be served promptly and with strict attention to their needs.

After an experience of more than fifteen years in the manufacture and sale of Gasolene, during which time we have furnished probably four-fifths of the entire quantity consumed in this market, we fully understand the requirements of customers, and respectfully solicit the patronage of those who desire strictly reliable goods.

Pratt's Double Distilled & Deodorized Naphthas.

The attention of all who use any of these goods in the arts and manufactures is invited to our own products, of the various gravities, from 62° to 76° Beaumé, inclusive. These are prepared with the greatest care, and will be found especially desirable for manufacturers of Varnishes, Mixed Paints, Oil-cloths, Rubber and Enamel Goods, Window-shades, etc.; also for Druggists' use, and every purpose requiring a perfectly pure and sweet article. We are prepared to furnish them in any quantity, by the single barrel or car-load, and are confident that all who are critical as to quality will be well pleased with them.

BOULEVARD GAS FLUID. — We distill a special grade of Naphtha (which we market under this name), for use in what are known as Naphtha or Vapor Burners, for street-lamps, a large number of which are now in use for lighting the streets of many cities and towns here and in foreign countries.

L'Envoy.

GO, *Little Book, to subtle world,*
    And show thy simple face,
And forward pass, and do not turn
    Again to our disgrace.
For thou shalt bring to people's ears
    But truth, that needs not blush;
And though perchance thou get'st rebuke,
    Care not for that a rush:
For evil tongues do itch so sore,
    They must be rubbing still
Against their teeth, that should hold fast
    The clapper of the mill.
Desire that man that likes thee not
    To lay thee down again,
Till some sweet nap and harmless sleep
    Hath settled troubled brain.

Press of Theo. L. De Vinne & Co. New-York.

A Paradise of Daintie Devices: A Collection of
Poems, Songs, and Ballads, by various hands. At
New-York: Imprinted for Charles Pratt & Co., at 46
Broadway, near Trinity Church-yard. *Christmas, 1882.*

Opinions of the Press.

"Advertising has become a literary art. Charles Pratt & Co. have prepared for circulation among their customers in the oil trade an excellent
collection of poems, songs, and ballads. Printed on heavy paper with
broad margins, and furnished with an enticing title, 'A Paradise of Daintie
Devices,' it is an artistic souvenir for the holiday trade." * * * * *
—*New-York Tribune, Dec. 13, 1882.*

"A beautiful little volume, bearing the quaint and not modern title of 'A
Paradise of Daintie Devices,' is published by Charles Pratt & Co., oil manu-
facturers. It contains poems, ancient and modern, English, Irish, and
American, selected with taste and printed in a fitting manner. It is an
agreeable and curious product of the Christmas season."—*New-York Sun,
Dec. 13, 1882.*

"The 'æsthetic' devices of tradesmen to attract attention are usually so
odious that one is ready to forget the advertising purpose of so pretty, well-
chosen, and well-printed a budget of verse as the 'Paradise of Daintie
Devices: A Collection of Poems, Songs, and Ballads,' distributed by Charles
Pratt & Co." * * * * * —*The Nation, Dec. 14, 1882.*

"One of the prettiest books of the season is an advertisement of Pratt's
Astral Oil, etc. 'A Paradise of Daintie Devices' it is called—the daintiest
device being the harmless deception practiced upon the reader. It is a well-
chosen collection of poems, songs, and ballads, dating from Richard Crashaw
to T. B. Aldrich; and it is printed in Francis Hart & Co's best style."—
The Critic, Dec. 16, 1882.

"Æsthetics in advertising can go no arther. 'A Paradise of Daintie Devices,' which is a choicely culled selection of ' Poems, Songs, and Ballads,' is done up in an ordinary stiff brown-paper cover, but so quaintly entitled thereon, with ornamental initials, and head and tail piece, that the eye is at once pleasantly attracted. The contents prove to include many poetical favorites, and some selections not familiar, but all in good taste and discovering proper critical judgment. The reader is, however, astounded when, on reaching the last pages, he discovers that the whole undertaking is a Christmas gift from Charles Pratt & Co., manufacturers of oil. And truly a most suitable and symbolical recognition of the amount of oil — Pratt's Astral, and other, of the midnight species more particularly — that has been burned in the cause of literature."—*The American Bookseller, Dec. 15, 1882.*

"A very unique publication is a 'Paradise of Daintie Devices,' being a collection of Poems, Songs, and Ballads, by various hands. It contains a few standard poems by well-known authors, with several ancient and some modern ballads, and is very cleverly got up in antique style. It bears the following imprint: ' At New-York: Imprinted for Charles Pratt & Co., at 46 Broadway, near Trinity Church-yard. Christmas, 1882.' "—*New-York Observer, Dec. 21, 1882.*

"Astral oil has had its chief claim on literature in the light it shed on the student; but this winter it has shone out over ' A Paradise of Daintie Devices,' issued by Charles Pratt & Co. to their friends and customers. The wide-margined, rough-edged, brown-covered, antique-typed anthology of 102 small quarto pages which bears this title is, take it all in all, one of the aptest, as it is one of the costliest, advertisements ever indulged in by a firm whose choice of this method is, in its way, an equal compliment to the perceptions of its patrons and proof of its own high taste. It is surprising, when one remembers the senseless sums wasted on lithographing of all orders and colors, that this dainty device of enlisting the best of literature in the service has never before been adopted."—*Philadelphia Press, Dec. 22, 1882.*

"'A Paradise of Daintie Devices,' etc. Although issued gratuitously as a souvenir to the patrons of the publishers, this is an unique specimen of bookmaking; it is gotten up in antique style, with quaint head and tail pieces, printed on fine linen paper, with broad margin and uncut edges. It contains some charming poems and ballads from the early poets, and also from modern writers."—*The Publishers' Weekly, New-York, January 13, 1883.*

"A beautiful little volume, bearing the uncommon title of 'A Paradise of Daintie Devices,' is published by Charles Pratt & Co., oil manufacturers. It is curious, quaint, and æsthetic to a degree."—*Brooklyn (N. Y.) Eagle.*